PUGWASH
AND THE
BURIED
TREASURE

236736

A Pirate Story by

JOHN RYAN

for LAURA

THE BODLEY HEAD

LONDON

It was a dark and
stormy night; a great
gale blew and the *Black
Pig* was tossed high and
low by the mountainous
waves which broke across
the Caribbean Sea.

The pirates were all down below, clinging to their hammocks and feeling dreadfully sea-sick. All, that is, except for two . . .

Tom the cabin boy was up on deck at the wheel, fighting to keep the ship into the wind. And, strangely enough, Captain Pugwash was up there too . . .

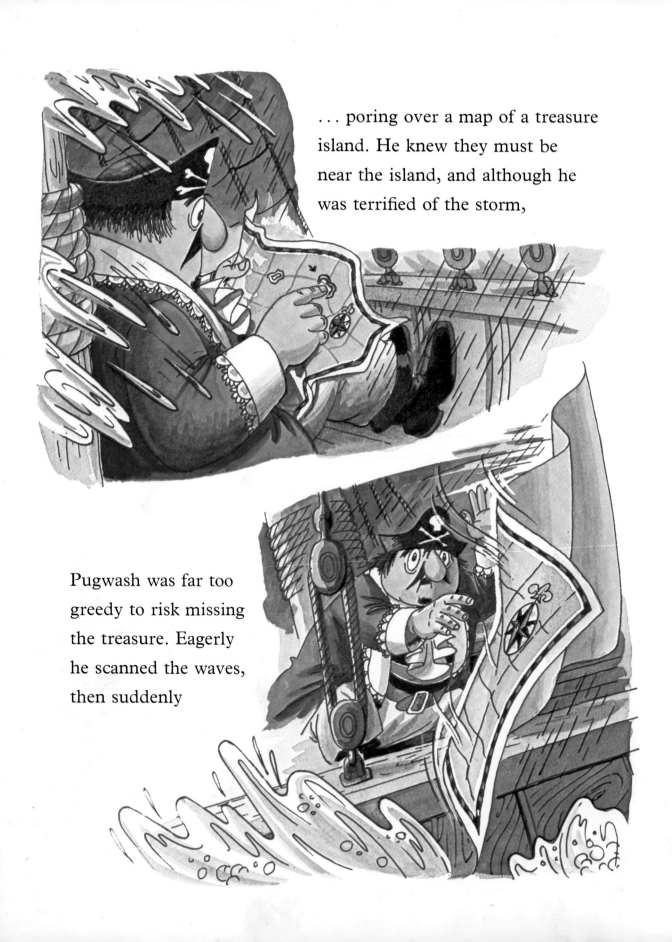

... poring over a map of a treasure island. He knew they must be near the island, and although he was terrified of the storm,

Pugwash was far too greedy to risk missing the treasure. Eagerly he scanned the waves, then suddenly a gust of wind snatched the map from his grasp

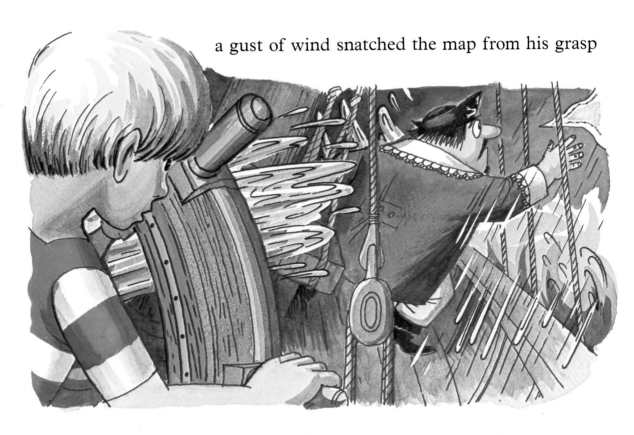

and as he started after it a great wave caught him

and swept him off his feet,

tossing him over the
side of the ship into
the raging waves below.

Poor Captain Pugwash! He hated cold water and he was a very poor swimmer. And he knew that in a storm like this even Tom wouldn't be able to turn the ship back to save him.

By now the *Black Pig* was
disappearing into the darkness
and Pugwash felt that his
last hour really had come.
Then all of a sudden ...

... his hand struck something hard. LAND! It wasn't dry land but it was at least firm. In the darkness the Captain could just see the outline of a tiny rocky island. Desperately he dragged himself up on to it, and a moment later ... he fell into an exhausted sleep.

When the Captain awoke it was dawn. The
terrible storm was over, the sea was dead calm.
And there he sat, all alone on his little island.
Or *was* he alone?

From close by, on the other side of the rock in fact, he heard a snore . . .

... then a loud SNORT.
And he knew that snort
all too well. He looked
round, and yes ...
there to his horror
and terror

sat his worst and most dreaded enemy, the wickedest and most ferocious pirate on the seven seas, Cut-throat Jake! Then Pugwash got another surprise ...

Cut-throat Jake was smiling!

At first of course the Captain was absolutely *terrified*

but oddly enough, Cut-throat Jake seemed friendly.
He told Pugwash how he too had been swept away
by the storm and cast up on the island.

And very soon the two pirates were chatting away just like old friends.

D'YE REMEMBER THE TIME WHEN...

GO ON, TAKE IT.... DO!

Pugwash even shared his last bit of sea-watery chocolate with his old enemy.

THANK'EE SO MUCH!!

At least he *pretended* it was his last piece of chocolate, and Cut-throat Jake *pretended* that he believed him!

Then, far away on the horizon, they saw a
ship. Both pirates were very excited. "Why, ain't
that lucky now that we've become mates!" said Jake.

"With the two of us it'll be easy to attract their
attention! Take yer jacket off, me handsome!"

Jake stood on the rock and Pugwash climbed on to his shoulders and waved his coat wildly.

And the ship seemed to be getting closer . . . and closer . . . and closer, although in the early morning light it was difficult to be absolutely sure.

Captain Pugwash was beginning to feel rather dizzy so finally both pirates stood hand in hand on their little island and shouted for all they were worth.

Soon the ship was so close that Cut-throat Jake
roared with delight and gave a blood-thirsty
chuckle. "Why!" he growled, "it's me own ship
the *Flyin' Dustman*, and me own shipmates come
to save me. Ho, Ho!"

"And me too?" asked Pugwash nervously.

AHOY THERE CAP'N JAKE!

"Save *you*?" roared Jake. "You didn't *believe* all that clap-trap about 'bygones be bygones' did 'ee? That was just to get 'ee to help me make 'em see us! Nay! It's *me* that's for savin' and *you* that's for maroonin' on this 'ere island, aharrh!"

FLYING DUSTMAN

By this time Jake's pirates had arrived in their long-boat. And a moment later Cut-throat Jake was being helped aboard.

"B-b-but you can't *leave* me here!" cried Pugwash.

"Why that I can and that I *will*, you old scallywag," replied Jake.

And he was gone, and very soon the *Flying Dustman* was receding into the distance.

"Come back! Come BACK!" shouted Captain Pugwash. But Jake and his crew only laughed at him. And very soon the Captain couldn't even hear that.

As the hot mid-day sun rose overhead and
Jake's ship disappeared over the eastern horizon,
poor Captain Pugwash gave up all hope. In fact,
he was so hopeless and downcast he never noticed
that over the *western* horizon *another* ship had
arrived.

It was the Captain's ship, the *Black Pig*!

Eagerly the pirates rushed to the side.

In next to no time Tom the cabin boy was on his way to the tiny island in the dinghy. "Well done, Tom lad!" cried Pugwash. "I might have known none of you would rest until you had found your gallant Captain!"

"Well, as a matter of fact," said Tom, "it wasn't *you* we were looking for."

"We found your map after the storm; it was caught in the rigging. And with the map we found the island. And as for the treasure Cap'n, why . . .

YOU'VE BEEN SITTING ON IT!''

And sure enough
they found

under the rocks
and sand

an ancient rusty chest,

which was absolutely *stuffed* with treasure!

That night they all had a very merry party
aboard the *Black Pig*. As the pirates played with
the sparkling loot and counted it all up, Captain
Pugwash told them *his* version of the story:

– how he had cleverly spotted the island in the storm, dived into the raging sea, swam ashore and took possession of the island, defending it against Cut-throat Jake, and finally how he had driven off Jake and his entire villainous crew!

"I just don't know *what* you'd do without me,"
remarked Captain Pugwash later as Tom
prepared his bath.

"Hm, I felt we did pretty well on our own,"
thought Tom, "but even so, it's good to have our
Cap'n back again!"

First published in 1980 by The Bodley Head Ltd
This edition published in 1993 by
The Bodley Head Children's Books
An imprint of Random House UK Limited
20 Vauxhall Bridge Road, London SW1V 2SA
Printed in Hong Kong
ISBN 0 370 30338 5